D1001511

Two Mice in New York: A Holiday Adventure

Written by Donna Dalton
Illustrated by David Pfendler

Love and peace,
Donna Dalton

Creative Minds Publications
Richmond, Virginia

ISBN: 978-0-578-65146-0
Library of Congress Control Number: 2020904801

Printed in the United States

Published by Creative Minds Publications
Richmond, Virginia
www.creativemindspublications.com

Previous Books by
Donna Dalton

Two Mice at the Eiffel Tower
Two Mice in London

This book is dedicated to
my sweet grandchildren,
Tyler and Kinsley.

May you always have HOPE, LOVE,
JOY, PEACE, and GOODWILL
in your life, not just during the
holidays, but all throughout the year.
DeeDee loves you to New York City and back!

Thank you to my sister, Linda, and my
many Two Mice readers who suggested
ideas for *Two Mice in New York:
A Holiday Adventure.*

Azura and Afrodille arrive early on a Monday morning in November to meet Madame Bella at the bench by the Eiffel Tower. They can hardly wait for their winter trip to New York City to celebrate the upcoming holiday season.

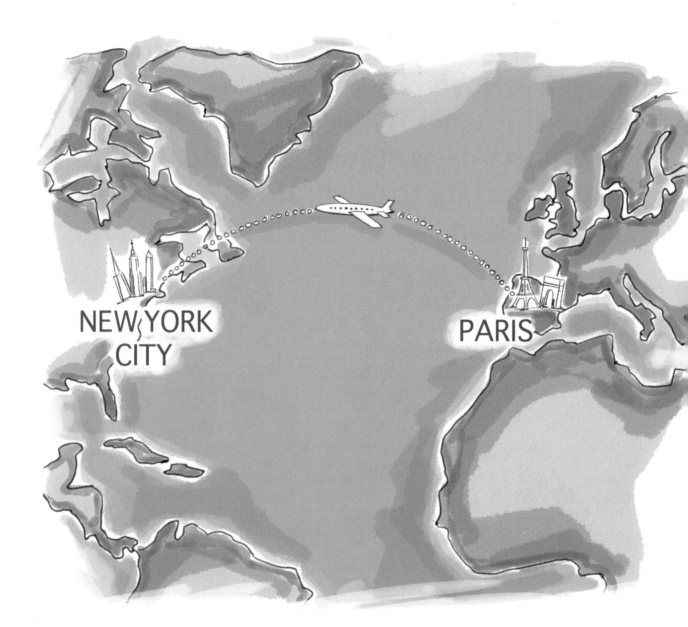

The two mice are excited to travel by airplane across the magnificent Atlantic Ocean, the second largest of the world's five oceans. Once they arrive in the big city, they will travel by trains, subways, and the famous bright yellow taxi cabs to visit the sights of the bustling city that never sleeps.

On the flight, Azura and Afrodille quiz each other on facts about New York City.
How many people live in New York City?
How many languages are spoken there?
How large is New York City? What are some of the famous nicknames for the city?
Madame Bella laughs at their rapid-fire question and answer game.

After landing in "The Big Apple," Madame Bella, Azura, and Afrodille head toward their hotel overlooking Times Square which is brightly lit by giant billboards and advertisements. What a busy place! The two mice are amazed by the thousands of people on the streets.

Tomorrow will be a huge day for the two mice and Madame Bella. They are going to the Macy's Thanksgiving Day Parade, the world's largest parade.

The Macy's Thanksgiving Day Parade is the kick-off event to the wonderful holiday season celebrated in New York City. The parade features floats, cheerleaders, dancers, clowns, and even marching bands. The two mice wake up very early to claim their spot on the street to watch the parade. It's Thanksgiving Day!

Madame Bella lifts Azura and Afrodille high into the air to give them a better view and keep the two mice from being squashed. The two mice cannot believe their eyes when they see GIANT helium-filled balloons floating through the air carried by volunteers holding on to them with long ropes.

A gust of cold wind comes along threatening to blow away the oldest balloon, Felix the Cat. Azura and Afrodille jump from Madame Bella's hands. Each one grabs a rope to help the volunteers save the humongous cat from blowing away. The crowd cheers at the bravery and irony of the two mice saving the cat.

After the parade ends, the two mice stop
by street vendors to nibble on bites of pizza
and big pretzels. The two mice believe these
tasty treats are much better than turkey
and dressing, a usual Thanksgiving meal.
The two mice are having such an exciting day
that they are not prepared for what happens
next.

When they return to the hotel in Times Square, the two mice and Madame Bella are astounded to see the electronic billboard flashing an urgent message to the citizens and visitors of New York.

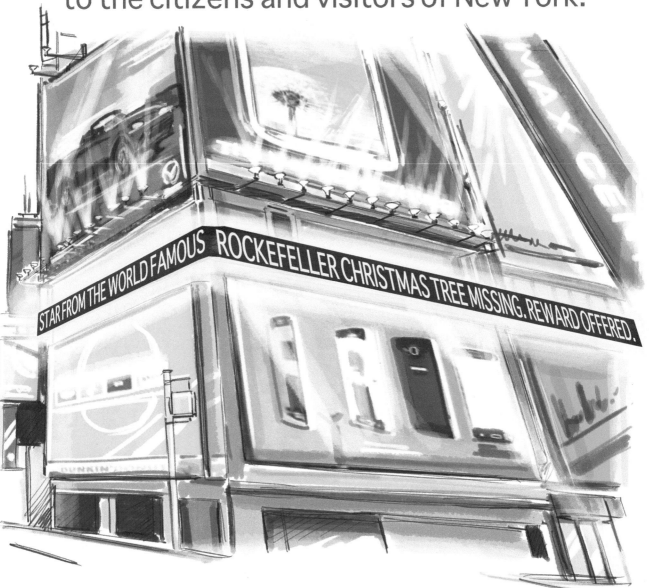

STAR FROM THE WORLD FAMOUS ROCKEFELLER CHRISTMAS TREE MISSING. REWARD OFFERED.

"The lighting of the tree is less than a week away," Afrodille exclaims. "We must find the star!"

A few days ago, this year's 100-foot tree was cut down outside the city and transported on a large truck to Rockefeller Center. The workers labored day and night on cranes to raise, stabilize, and decorate the tree. When they were placing the strings of lights on the tree, they quickly realized the star for the top of the tree was missing.

Without the star, the tree that visitors come from all over the world to see will not be the same. Azura and Afrodille know that they must find the missing star and save the lighting of the tree. After all, they had just saved a giant cat balloon from floating away! With only a few days left to find the star, where should they start looking?

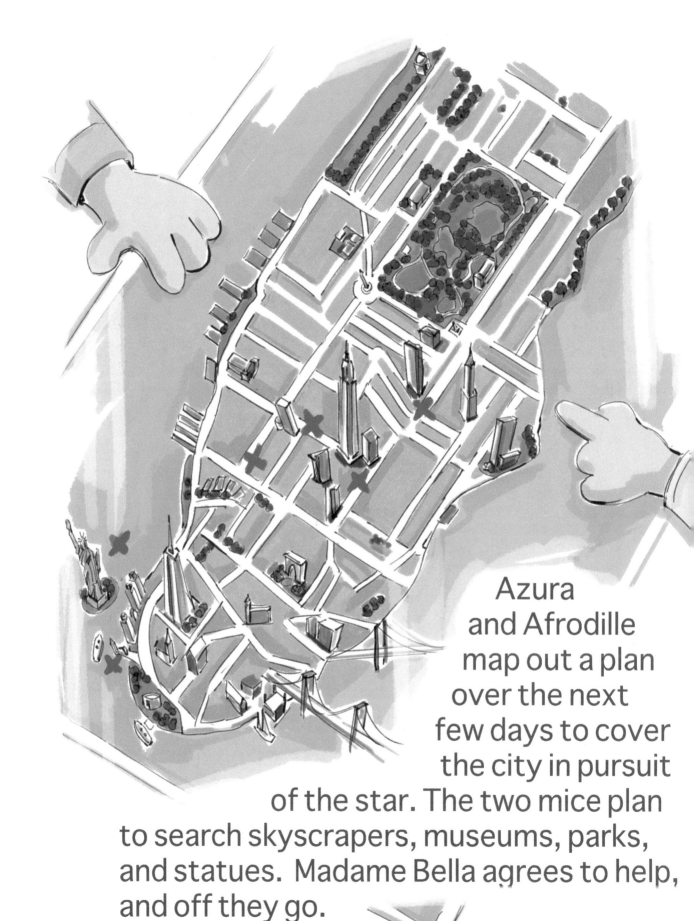

Azura and Afrodille map out a plan over the next few days to cover the city in pursuit of the star. The two mice plan to search skyscrapers, museums, parks, and statues. Madame Bella agrees to help, and off they go.

The first stop is the Statue of Liberty, a symbol of freedom. Madame Bella reminds the two mice that the Statue of Liberty was France's gift to America. Built in 1886, the Statue of Liberty is one of the largest statues standing at 305 feet tall. "Lady Liberty," as it is sometimes called, holds a torch above her crowned head with her right hand and a tablet inscribed with Roman numerals declaring the date of the Declaration of Independence in her left hand.

Next, Madame Bella and the two mice board a boat for a short ride to Ellis Island Immigration Museum to learn the stories of why people from other countries immigrated to America.

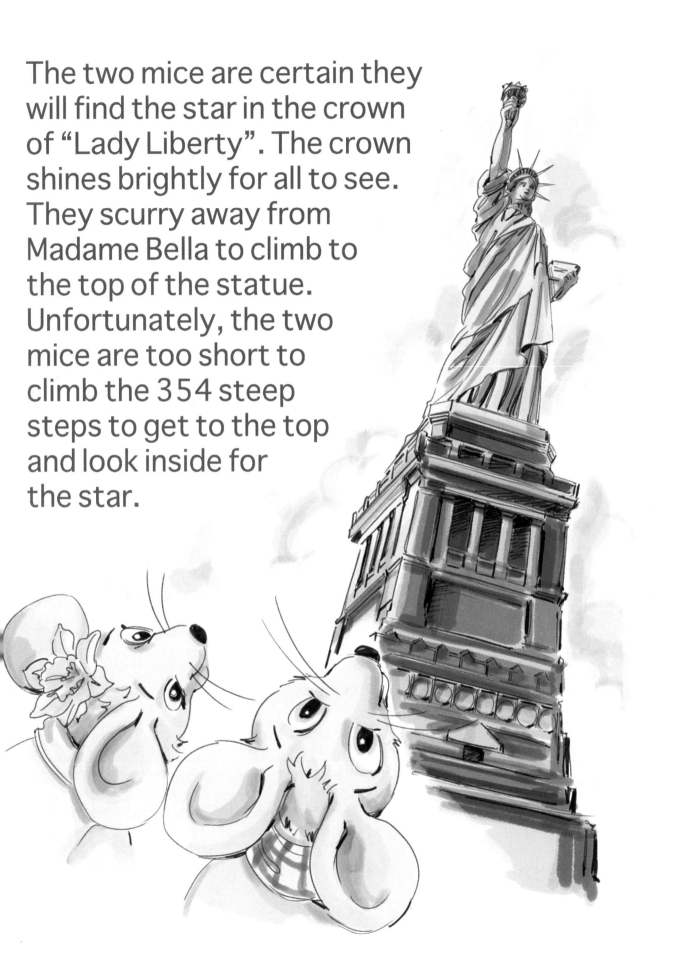

The two mice are certain they will find the star in the crown of "Lady Liberty". The crown shines brightly for all to see. They scurry away from Madame Bella to climb to the top of the statue. Unfortunately, the two mice are too short to climb the 354 steep steps to get to the top and look inside for the star.

Just then, Azura and Afrodille remember that after the parade they picked up one of the ropes tied to a giant balloon. They just figured it would come in handy for jump roping. Azura pulls the rope from Madame Bella's pocketbook, coils it, then uses his best lasso skills to hurl the rope around one of the points on "Lady Liberty's" crown.

While Azura holds one end of the rope, Afrodille carefully hoists herself up the rope all the way to the crown. Azura yells to Afrodille, "Don't look down!" Once inside the crown, Azura searches for the missing star. No luck.

Instead, she finds a piece of paper with the word HOPE scribbled on it. What does this mean? Is it a clue? She puts the paper in her side pocket and scales back down to the ground.

The two mice are disappointed that they did not find the star but have another plan. They decide to visit Central Park, a huge 2.5-mile park in the middle of the city. Maybe they will find the star hiding there.

Today the park trails are slippery. It is snowing! Madame Bella and her two furry friends hop onto a carriage guided by a horse adorned with a colorful coat and flowers. The three snuggle under a plaid blanket and begin their trip through the snowy park. CLIP, CLOP, CLIP, CLOP.

They hear the loud steps of the horse's hooves as they ride around the park. Azura and Afrodille see families and friends throwing snowballs, building snowmen, and catching the first snowflakes of winter on their tongues. They do not find the star. Instead, they discover the sounds of JOY that fill the park. Could this be another clue? Where should they look next?

At the edge of
Central Park,
Madame Bella,
Azura, and Afrodille
discover a life-size
nativity scene
near the Plaza Hotel.
The two mice gaze at
the Star of Bethlehem.
Could this be the star they are searching for?
They can't just remove the Star of Bethlehem
from the manger. It was this star that guided
the wisemen to find baby Jesus in the manger.
Suddenly, Azura and Afrodille spot two
children in the snow beside
the manger. They
are moving their
arms up and down
to make snow angels.
One of the children
writes the word LOVE
between the two snow
angels. Is this word
yet another clue to
finding the star?

Nearby, the two mice are amazed to see one of the world's largest menorahs. Erected to celebrate Hanukkah, the 32-foot tall, gold-colored, 4,000-pound steel menorah was assembled to celebrate the Jewish Festival of Lights. One light will be lit each of the eight nights to celebrate Hanukkah. Azura and Afrodille are in awe of the many lights that adorn the menorah. But, there is still no sign of the star.

Just beyond the menorah, Madame Bella, Azura, and Afrodille spot a man holding a very large poster of a John Lennon quote. What a great message for the season and spirit of the holidays. Is this another sign?

Madame Bella decides to go back to the hotel to rest her feet from a busy day of sightseeing, but not Azura and Afrodille. They decide to hail a yellow taxi to the Empire State Building, standing 1,454 feet tall. The skyscraper has many windows, lights, and two observation decks on the 86th and 102nd floors. Certainly, the star would be found here! Unfortunately, animals are not allowed in the elevators. What are they going to do?

Then, Azura remembers that his cousin Frankie lives deep under the streets in the subways of New York City.

Frankie is a big, furry rat with long whiskers but also has the biggest smile, bright green eyes, and a giant heart.

Azura and Afrodille head down to the nearest subway station in search of Frankie. Frankie is a native New Yorker. He will know exactly what to do!

Running down the stairs onto the subway platform, Azura and Afrodille see lots of friendly rats. They send a message to Frankie.

When Frankie arrives, he has his rat pack in tow, and they are ready to help. Azura, Afrodille, Frankie, and the rat pack quickly scamper back to the Empire State Building. By linking arms and standing on each other's shoulders, Frankie and his team build a pyramid of rats and are able to boost the two mice to an open window.
They sneak in and begin to search room by room for the star. It's not here either.
Azura and Afrodille thank the rat pack for their GOODWILL and kind efforts in supporting the quest for the lost star.

Azura and Afrodille are so disappointed that they have not discovered the missing star. They drift off to sleep that night with visions of today's events circling in their minds - the word HOPE scribbled on a piece of paper in the Statue of Liberty, the sound of JOY in Central Park, the word LOVE written between two snow angels, the giant menorah and the nearby sign of PEACE, and the GOODWILL of Frankie and his rat pack. Could all of these clues lead to the missing star?

HOPE

IMAGINE ALL THE PEOPLE LIVING LIFE IN PEACE

The two mice wake up the next morning with a burst of creativity. While they have not yet found the star, the two mice know what they need to do. Azura and Afrodille send Madame Bella to the nearby store to find paper, pens, scissors, and colorful trinkets. Then, the three companions work together to create a unique star with five special words, HOPE, LOVE , JOY, PEACE, and GOODWILL, one on each of the points. Each clue describes the spirit of the holiday season celebrated every year in the city.

The following morning, Madame Bella, Azura, and Afrodille hurry to the Rockefeller Center Christmas Tree. Azura and Afrodille step onto the landing of the giant crane, which lifts them to the top of the 100-foot tree.

This time, Afrodille shouts to Azura, "Don't look down!" The two mice proudly place the homemade star on top of the tree.

The citizens of New York are so excited to see a new star for the magnificent tree. As the reward for creating a new star, the mayor invites Madame Bella, Afrodille, Azura, and Frankie to the special lighting of the tree. With the help of thousands of visitors, the countdown begins ... ten, nine, eight, seven, six, five, four, three, two, one ... the four companions pull the switch to illuminate the colorful lights and the brand new star! Cheers of "Merry Christmas" and "Happy Holidays" ring out among the crowd.

Over 125 million visitors travel to New York City each year to see the amazing tree, and this year is no exception. People stop and reflect on the true meaning of the words, HOPE, LOVE, JOY, PEACE, and GOODWILL, found on the star. Visitors begin to hang their own decorated stars on the tree with more words such as HAPPINESS, GIVING, WONDER, and LAUGHTER. What words would you put on your star?

The celebration continues around the tree well into the night. Azura and Afrodille join the world-famous dancers, the Rockettes, as they dance around the tree kicking their feet high into the air in a synchronized fashion to the rhythm of "Jingle Bells."

Madame Bella then takes the two mice over to the famous skating rink in Rockefeller Center. Azura and Afrodille have never been ice skating. They hold on to each other as they skate around the rink trying so hard not to fall.

They stop for hot chocolate and marshmallows as they travel back to the hotel.

Madame Bella tucks the two exhausted mice into bed that night and gives them a kiss. In the days ahead, the mice continue to tour around the city enjoying museums, shops, plays, and a few more special sights. The holiday trip to New York City will officially come to an end when the giant crystal ball drops in Times Square, signaling the new year.

Azura and Afrodille
fall asleep dreaming of
their next adventure.
Where do you think
the two mice and
Madame Bella should
travel next?

CPSIA information can be obtained
at www.ICGtesting.com
Printed in the USA
BVHW022040120520
578508BV00001B/1